First published in Great Britain in 2010 by Simon and Schuster UK Ltd,
a CBS company.

Text copyright © 2010 Tamsyn Murray
Cover and interior illustrations copyright © 2010 Lee Wildish

Simon & Schuster UK Ltd
1st Floor, 222 Gray's Inn Road, London WC1X 8HB

This book is a work of fiction. Names, characters, places and incidents are either the product of the author's imagination or are used fictitiously. Any resemblance to actual people living or dead, events or locales is entirely coincidental.

A CIP catalogue record for this book is available from the British Library.

978-1-84738-727-1

1 3 5 7 9 10 8 6 4 2

Printed and bound in Great Britain.

www.simonandschuster.co.uk

www.tamsynmurray.co.uk

STUNT BUNNY

SHOWBIZ SENSATION

TAMSYN MURRAY

ILLUSTRATED BY LEE WILDISH

For Ronnie and Roxie, the original Stunt Bunnies

CHAPTER ONE

Introducing Harriet Houdini

I'll let you into a secret. My name hasn't always been Harriet Houdini. For about twenty minutes after Susie and her dad brought me home from the pet shop, I was called Flopsy. Have you ever heard anything so ridiculous in your life? I may have the cutest little bunny ears and the fluffiest grey bunny tail but that doesn't mean I deserve a name like that. It tells you a lot about my family, the Wilsons – soppy, all of them.

Actually, that's not true. I don't have any problems with Susie. She's my owner and the sweetest eight-year-old I know. Don't be fooled by her big, blue eyes and angelic face, though – Susie is one smart cookie. She takes really good care of me and knows exactly how I like my cabbage. And if she hadn't begged for a birthday bunny and picked me out of all the other rabbits at Noah's Ark pet shop, who knows where I'd have ended up? Mrs Wilson, Susie's mum, is OK. She can be a bit bossy but, as long as she doesn't tell me what to do, we get along fine. Then there's Lily, Susie's naughty little sister.

The less said about her, the better, but even she's not as bad as their dad. I call him Evil Edward – EE for short. He doesn't like me and I can't think why. OK, there *may* have been a small accident when we first met involving his finger and my teeth but nothing serious. I mean, there was hardly any blood. You'd think I'd taken his finger off the way he went on.

'It bit me!' he yelled, dragging his hand out of the cardboard box I was in. 'I knew we should have chosen that white rabbit. He didn't look half as savage.'

Susie stopped spreading sawdust on

the bottom of the brand-new hutch they'd bought and hurried over. 'You must have scared her. Poor Flopsy!'

'Poor Flopsy?' EE growled. 'Poor me, more like.'

With one last glare, he closed the lid of the box, leaving me in the dark.

Now, I don't know about you but I don't like being shut in anywhere. A nice, comfortable hutch is fine. A cramped box isn't, so I did what anyone would do. I escaped.

The cardboard was no match for my set of trusty teeth. No one noticed me poking my velvet nose through the hole I'd chewed, they were too busy fussing around the tiny scratch on EE's finger. With a twitch of my whiskers, I was off, hopping across the grass and into the open garden shed before they noticed I was gone. Only Smudge, the family cat, saw me go and he just blinked and yawned.

You should have heard them when they finally opened the box and found I wasn't there.

'She's gone!' exclaimed Susie's mum.

'Where did that hole come from?' EE said.

'Where is she?' Susie's voice wobbled.

'Bye bye, bunny,' Lily said.

It was ages before anyone thought of looking in the shed. And, even though I had squeezed in tightly between a smelly cat basket and a tatty, old sun lounger, they found me in the end.

'Oh, Flopsy, you bad bunny!' Susie cried, burying her face in my soft, grey fur. 'Don't ever do that again.'

Just as I was starting to feel the teeniest bit guilty, EE said, 'After an escape like that we should be calling

11

it Harry Houdini.'

Susie looked confused. 'Who?'

'Harry Houdini,' he repeated. 'He was famous magician who escaped from all kinds of impossible places, a bit like Flopsy here.'

Hands on hips, Susie said, 'She's a *girl*. We can't call her Harry.'

'How about Harriet, then?'

So, that's how I came to be called Harriet Houdini. With a name like that, life was never going to be boring.

CHAPTER TWO
Does My Bum Look Big In This?

I soon worked out that Susie's little sister can be Trouble with a capital T. At five years old, Lily is into teddy bears in a big way. If it's furry, she cuddles it. Which is obviously a problem for me! Don't get me wrong, I really like snuggling on the sofa after a hard day in the hutch, but no way do I want to be squashed up against Lily's sticky face. Then there's what she does to her teddies. Trust me; a frilly doll's dress is *not* a good look for a polar bear.

Luckily for me, Susie is very strict where I'm concerned and Lily is never allowed to let me out unless she's there. So, when Lily got chickenpox and Susie didn't, I wasn't worried. Lily might have ten days off school with nothing much to do, but that didn't bother me. She knew that opening the hutch door on her own was forbidden, right?

Wrong. Whilst Susie's mum was chatting to a neighbour at the front door,

Lily was busy twisting open the locks on my cage and smuggling me upstairs under her jumper. Before I knew it, I was wearing a lacy bonnet and getting a very bad feeling about what was coming next.

'Hawwit has come for tea,' she told Smudge in a stern voice, as he tried to sneak away from the pretend picnic in front of us. 'Play nice with her.'

Smudge, who had a bright pink ribbon tied around his neck, which didn't go with his amber eyes at all, looked like he wished he was somewhere else and I knew exactly how he felt. Any moment now, Lily would decide I needed a dress

15

to go with the bonnet and I would be up to my paws in pink.

At least I didn't have much to do; Lily was happy doing all the talking. I wasn't even really listening until a few key words made my ears prick up. *Vicar? Church?* I looked up to see Lily heading my way, holding a white dress and the full horror hit me. She was

playing at weddings and if Barbie was the bridesmaid and Smudge was the groom, there was only one person missing from the picture. The bride!

Well, I wasn't having any of that. Quick as a flash, I leaped across the floor and wriggled to safety under the chest of drawers.

'Bad Hawwit!' Lily's fingers poked after me, as she squashed her face into

the gap between the carpet and the bottom drawer. 'You're going to be late for the church.'

I pressed against the wall and got comfy. With a bit of luck, she'd get bored and I could escape. Sure enough, I heard Susie's mum calling and Lily wandered off with Smudge under her arm, forgetting all about me.

Making sure the coast was clear, I squeezed out into the middle of the room. The plan was to hop down the stairs and head out into the garden, where EE's best rosebushes were covered in tasty flowers. My mouth was watering at the thought of chomping on all those juicy petals.

Then I saw that Lily had shut the bedroom door on her way out. I ground my teeth together. Now I'd have to wait until she came back in and then make a break for it . . . or would I? The door handle wasn't *so* very far away. Maybe I could jump high enough to reach it.

Crouching down low, I pushed hard into the

floor and leaped towards the handle. My claws scrabbled on the metal for a second and then I was back on the carpet – which wasn't as soft as it looked. I tried again. It was no use, the handle wasn't budging. What I really needed was a trampoline, but as the only one was in the garden downstairs, it was on to Plan B – wait for Lily. Except she didn't come back for ages! Susie's mum took her to collect Susie from school and by the time they came home, I'd fallen asleep next to Barbie, who didn't seem to care that she wasn't going to be a bridesmaid after all. And that's where Susie found me, after another frantic search, still in my bonnet.

'Blasted animal,' EE muttered darkly, as he fitted a padlock to the door of the hutch. 'Let's see if you're so clever once you've had your claws clipped next week.'

Honestly, I don't know what his problem is. This time it really wasn't my fault.

CHAPTER THREE

The Bunny Doctor

I should have known something was up when the cat basket came out of the shed. Smudge knew; one look at it and he was off, over the fence and into next-door's garden with his furry tail firmly between his legs. But no one batted an eyelid. They crowded around my hutch instead and EE had a determined expression on his face.

'I don't want any slip ups,' he said, sounding like an army sergeant. 'We're due at the Vee Eee Tee at 5.30 and I'm not spending half an hour chasing a loose rabbit first.'

Who was he calling loose? And did he really think that by spelling it out I wouldn't know what he was saying? Susie must get all her brains from her mum.

To prove him wrong, I didn't even wriggle when Susie lifted me into the cat basket and sat perfectly still as she fastened the buckles on the door.

I was as good as gold for the whole car journey into the town and I didn't make a sound as the vet poked and prodded me.

'I must say, she's very well behaved,' the vet said, glancing up at EE and Susie as he trimmed my nails – I tried not to mind, even though it had taken me ages to grow them that long.

'It's all an act,' EE replied, with a suspicious glance down at me. 'Can you do that to her teeth? She ate half my slipper last week.'

The vet looked confused. 'She's a rabbit, Mr Wilson.

24

It's what they do, I'm afraid.'

EE frowned. 'She keeps escaping too.'
Chuckling, the vet said, 'Rabbits are naturally nosey. They like to get out and about.'

Call me oversensitive but it seemed the more the vet stood up for me, the less EE liked him. Although, after he'd stuck a giant needle into me, I decided I'd finally found something that EE and I agreed on. I mean, the vet said it was an important injection, but was there any need to push the needle in quite so hard? The back of my neck hurt for ages afterwards.

Back in the waiting room, they put my

basket on the floor while they waited to pay. To pass the time, I started to nibble the leather straps holding the basket door shut. They were old and it wasn't long before the bottom of the door was inviting me to push it open. The way I saw things, it would have been rude not to give it a nudge.

Plus, the waiting room was just begging to be explored. There were feet to sniff and other animals to meet. My nose twitched. What was that smell? Fresh hay? I squeezed under the door of the cat basket and hopped around the counter to investigate.

Before I could reach the hay, a Labrador

26

puppy spotted me and bounded over to 'play'. Let me tell you, being nudged on the bottom by a cold, wet nose isn't my idea of fun! So, I did what any self-respecting bunny would do – I ran for it.

The puppy chased me, yapping in excitement. Her owner squeaked and ran after her.

'Harriet!' Susie shouted, racing across the room.

And suddenly everyone was yelling at the top of their voices. Dogs barked, cats yowled and people rushed around trying to calm everything down. I watched the chaos from my hiding place under a display of pet food, which was the perfect hiding place . . . until the puppy saw me. Tail wagging, she jumped at me and all the bags of food.

The next bit happened in slow motion. Above me, the display wobbled and tipped sideways. People and pets stopped what they were doing to watch as the food-filled bags hit the water

cooler with an enormous *crash*. The big see-through bottle on top of the cooler flew into the air, spraying water all over the waiting room.

Everyone squealed as they got soaked, but that wasn't the end of it. Some of the water must have hit one of the computers because there was a loud

bang and a *flash* and the lady behind the counter jumped backwards, with a worried-sounding scream.

'What on earth is going on out here?' The door of the vet's room slammed open and he stamped out, his face looking like a big, black thunder cloud.

Everything went quiet.

'Harriet escaped,' Susie said, in a small voice that made me feel very bad indeed. There was a sudden fizzing noise from behind the desk. 'And . . . I think your computer might be broken.'

The vet looked at the dripping waiting room, with its soggy animals and owners. 'I see,' he rumbled, taking a deep breath. 'And where is Harriet now?'

You could have heard a pin drop when I shuffled out. Every pair of eyes watched as I hopped across to the cat basket and wriggled inside.

'I told you so,' EE said to the vet, in a way which made me think he enjoyed saying it.

'Get that rabbit out of here before she does any more damage,' the vet said, pointing a shaking finger at the door.

EE seemed strangely cheerful on the way out to the car. 'I think that went quite well, don't you?' he said, beaming at Susie. 'What a shame we didn't have a camera. I bet there are TV shows that would pay money for a fuss like that.'

Anyone would think he was pleased I'd escaped. I'm telling you, I will never understand him.

CHAPTER FOUR
The Best Magician in the World

Not every pet has got the cute factor. Some of them, like lizards and stick insects, just aren't very pretty. They probably have all sorts of other talents, just not the kind that win beauty contests. I, on the other hand, was born to look adorable. So, I can't say I was surprised when Susie announced she'd entered me in the children's pet show at our village church summer fair. What did confuse me was EE's attitude.

'Have you got Harriet's brush?' he asked Susie for the millionth time, peering into the cat basket like he thought I might have escaped. 'And the ribbon for around her neck?'

I didn't get it. If I didn't know better I'd say he was keener than Susie for me to win, which is more than could be said for Smudge, who was sitting by the window when we left, sulking. Secretly, I think he wished he was going to the pet show.

It was a sunny day and the village green was already crowded when we arrived. There was a Punch and Judy show, a candyfloss stall and a carousel with brightly painted horses. By the time Mrs Wilson and Lily went off to find the face-painting tent, Susie was practically jumping up and down with excitement.

'Oooh, can I go on the Helter Skelter please, Dad?'

EE shook his head. 'We need to get to the pet show. We wouldn't want to miss out on the fifty-pound prize by being late.'

So that was it. EE had his eye on the money I'd win for coming first. Well, we'd just see about that.

We hurried over to the judging arena. When I saw the other pets, I was sure the

prize was as good as mine. Among others, there was a parrot that shouted 'Bogies!' every five minutes, a cat with a face so squashed it looked like it had run into a window at full speed and a goldfish. I'm not kidding. George Green, our next-door neighbour, had entered his fish, believing it was going to out-cute the fluffy animals. He was going to be disappointed.

They all were. The shiny silver trophy for 'Best in Show' only had space for one name and that was mine.

'Dad, what's that for?' Susie was pointing at a sign not far from where we were waiting. Next to it was a tattered, red-and-white tent and an old table with a scruffy top hat on it.

'The Great Maldini's Conjuring Extravaganza,' EE read and snorted. 'It's some kind of magical mumbo-jumbo, I suppose. I'm not wasting money on that.'

George looked up from his goldfish. 'I bet it's rubbish.'

The front of the tent flew back and

a tall, thin man with a black, curly moustache appeared.

'Zere ees no better way to spend your money zan on zis magic show. I, ze Great Maldini, am ze best magician in ze world!'

EE looked at the man's wrinkled purple jacket and green bow tie. 'Then why isn't there a big crowd waiting to see your show?'

The Great Maldini scowled and waved a hand at me. 'Because zees idiots prefer to stare at ze animals zan come and see me.'

I could hardly believe my ears.

'That's right,' EE said, with a cheerful smile. 'Maybe you should get yourself a pet and join in.'

The Great Maldini hissed and snatched up his top hat. With one final glare at us, he whirled around and stamped into his tent, pulling it closed behind him.

'What a strange man,' Susie said.

'Weirdo,' George agreed. 'He probably doesn't even know any good tricks.'

'Never mind him, here come the judges,' EE said, grabbing my brush off the table and stuffing it underneath. 'Is that ribbon on straight?'

'Huh,' George said, shaking his head at us. 'You're going to need more than a ribbon to help you. Once Jaws here flaps his fins, your rabbit won't stand a chance.'

CHAPTER FIVE

Best in Show

George was wrong, because the judges loved me. At least, most of them did.

'Such bright eyes!' the lady judge exclaimed. A badge said her name was Mrs Peebles.

'What breed is she?' The second judge, a man, pushed his face close to mine.

'Netherland Dwarf,' Susie said proudly. 'Her name is Harriet Houdini.'

'How unusual,' said Mrs Peebles, with a smile. 'Why do you call her that?'

'Because she's always escaping.' The third judge's voice was grumpy. 'She caused a right rumpus in my surgery last week.'

Huh, just my luck – it was the vet who'd jabbed me. Seeing my chances of winning slipping away, I increased my cute appeal.

'Oh, how sweet! She's balancing on her hind legs,' Mrs Peebles exclaimed.

The first two judges scribbled away at their clipboards, but our vet didn't

write anything. Instead, he laid his
score sheet on the table and threw me a
suspicious look.

'You might want to get a collar and
lead,' he said to EE. 'Pet shops sell little
ones especially for rabbits.'

There was no way I was putting up

with that kind of nonsense. Next time they took me to the surgery he was in for a nip on the finger. In the meantime, I settled for leaving a little smelly present on his clipboard.

The judges were taking one final look at all the pets before going off to choose the winner. Now that I knew our vet was involved, I decided it was going to take an extra something to swing the votes my way. I was going to have to raise the cuteness factor if I wanted to take that trophy home.

Suddenly, I knew what I had to do . . . I waited until they were in front of me before I launched 'Operation Adorable'.

First of all, I cleaned my whiskers: no one can resist a bunny washing her face and these suckers were no exception.

'Isn't that the cutest thing you've ever seen?' The lady judge clapped her hands in delight.

'Hmmm,' said the vet.

I looked at him. He was a tough cookie, but he'd crumble soon enough. Wait until he got a load of my next move.

Carefully, I lifted myself on to my back legs and pushed upwards, soaring into a magnificent backflip. I landed neatly on the table, ears pointing straight upwards. For a second, no one moved.

46

Then applause burst out all around the table.

'Incredible!' Mrs Peebles had eyes like saucers.

'I've never seen anything like that before,' said the second judge.

Even our vet looked impressed. 'It's very unusual in a rabbit.'

All the clapping was attracting attention. People began coming over to see what the fuss was about. The Great Zucchini, or whatever he was called, came out of his tent and stood twirling his moustache as he watched. As the crowd grew, I decided it was time to seal the deal. Let them try and give first prize to anyone else.

I jumped again, even higher than before and this time did *two* graceful flips before landing. The roar of the crowd was enormous. I twitched my nose for extra cuteness.

'Well, I don't think there's any doubt about who the Best in Show trophy

should go to,' Mrs Peebles announced, with a stern look at the vet.

He didn't look happy, but he nodded in agreement. And that might have been the highlight of my day, if it wasn't for what happened next.

CHAPTER SIX

Stunt Bunny in Training

The must-see Saturday night TV show in the Wilson house was *Superpets*. Starring talented animals from all over the country; it was hosted by Gloria Goodwood. Over the last few weeks the show had been holding auditions to find Britain's best pet, the winner would get a big fat cash prize and would join the *Superpets* cast. And, although when the show was on I hopped around the living room pretending to ignore what was happening on the screen, secretly I was imagining it was me up there auditioning in front of Gloria and the other judges and winning the top spot on *Superpets*. It would never happen, of course. Everyone knew it was between Trevor's tumbling terrapins and Doodle the opera-singing poodle.

So, when I saw Gloria Goodwood pushing through the crowd towards me at the pet show, I couldn't believe my eyes. What was a big star like her doing in a tiny village like ours? I wasn't about to waste my only chance to impress her, though. Taking a deep breath, I waited until she had a clear view of me. My mouth was dry – I'd only have one shot at making her notice me. Swallowing, I closed my eyes and threw myself into what I can only describe as the most perfect *triple* bunny-flip ever seen.

Just as I'd planned, Gloria was hooked. 'That's an amazing trick,' she said, her eyes gleaming with interest.

'Does she do anything else?'

EE's face had gone a funny pink colour. 'Fnurg,' he mumbled, staring at Gloria with a star-struck expression.

'Dad!' Susie nudged him, cheeks rosy with embarrassment. 'I don't know if she can do any more tricks,' she said, turning to Gloria, 'but she can escape from almost anywhere. That's why we call her Harriet Houdini.'

A thoughtful look crossed Gloria's face.

'Harriet Houdini? I like it. She's exactly the kind of pet we need on the show.' She leaned down to study me. 'How would you like to be a celebrity, Harriet?'

I didn't need to be asked twice. Quicker than you could say 'crunchy carrots', I was up on my back legs and waving my front paws in excitement.

'I think that means "yes",' Gloria said, smiling. 'Stick with me, bunny. I'm going to make you a star!'

I couldn't wait to see the look on Smudge's face when he heard about this. He was going to be one unhappy kitty!

☆ ☆ ☆

Of course, there was a lot of paperwork to do, but I left that to Susie's mum and EE. As a celeb-to-be, I really couldn't be bothered with all the boring stuff and, besides, I was far too busy preparing my audition piece for *Superpets*.

I didn't make any special demands, but everyone at home knew I was a VIP. Susie invited all her friends round to fuss over me and they made glittery 'Showbiz Sensation' posters to take to the auditions. Lily tried to give my ears some extra sparkle using sequins and superglue, but Susie caught her just in time.

Smudge pretended not to care about all the attention I was getting, but I could see right through him. I hope he doesn't want to be an actor when he grows up, he's rubbish at it. Even EE showed me some respect when he saw how much I was going to be paid for appearing on the show.

'I don't earn that much in a week,' he moaned, looking at the numbers on the contract. 'All that for a few backflips?'

I didn't try to explain. To the untrained eye, a triple flip didn't seem hard, but that was because I made it look easy. No one was going to pay to see *him* do a backflip, were they? In fact, they wouldn't pay to see him do *anything*. What can I say? Either you've got the X-factor, or you haven't.

'Where did she learn to do that, anyway?' EE went on. 'It's not exactly normal bunny behaviour.'

He'd obviously never had to share

a home with fourteen other rabbits. When we'd been very young, the breeder had fed us by throwing handfuls of food high into the air. It was every bunny for herself – you had to grab some before it was all gone – and the best way to get a full tummy was to catch the food before it hit the ground. So, I'd learned to backflip and catch the scrummy pellets in mid-air. And now it looked as though my talent was starting to pay off. Things were on the up!

CHAPTER SEVEN

All Aboard the Superstar Express

'Are you sure you want to get the train to the city?' Mrs Wilson looked at me in the cat basket doubtfully 'I don't think Harriet is going to like it.'

EE folded his arms. 'She'll have to put up with it. There's nowhere to park near the *Superpets* studio.'

Actually, Susie's mum was wrong. I didn't mind getting the train. I could just see myself relaxing in the posh first-class seats, nibbling on an organic carrot. So, it was a bit of a shock when we pushed our way into the busy standard-class carriage and EE wedged my basket firmly under his seat.

'Let's see you get into trouble down there,' he said, looking at me with a smug smile.

It wasn't very comfortable on the floor. Every time the train went over a bump in the tracks, my basket jumped in the air and landed with a thud. So, it didn't take long for me to get cross.

Who did EE think he was dealing with? This was no way to prepare for the biggest moment of my life so far. Maybe *he* should sit on the floor so I could have *his* seat.

After a few more bone-shaking bumps, I'd really had enough! It was definitely time for one of my daring escapes. But, to stop me from nibbling through the straps on the basket, EE had tied thick string around the door, so it looked like I'd have to find another way out. I sniffed at the back of the basket and took a little nibble. It didn't taste too bad and I reckoned with a few chomps, I'd be out of there.

I got to work and soon made a hole big enough to wriggle through. Then I was off, hopping between the tatty trainers and scruffy sandals in search of a spare seat. I was almost at the end of the carriage before I found one. OK, so it wasn't *completely* empty, but I didn't mind sharing with a couple of coats.

It was a lot more comfortable up there,

in fact, it was so comfy that I must have dozed off because the next thing I knew, the ticket inspector was staring down at me.

'Is this your rabbit, Madam?' he asked the lady in the seat next to mine.

She let out a tiny squeal and jumped up. 'Oh, no, I can't stand furry little creatures!'

The ticket inspector looked at the man sitting opposite me. 'Is the bunny with you, Sir?'

The man shook his head. 'I've never seen it before in my life.'

With an ominous *click* of his ticket clipper, the inspector said, 'Then it seems we have a stowaway aboard the train. The police will want to know about this.'

He reached down to grab hold of me, but I was ready for him. Quicker than you could say, 'Tickets, please!' I was off and scampering away across the seats to freedom.

'Stop that bunny!' the inspector shouted and thudded along the carriage

behind me. Hands grabbed at my fur as I raced towards the safety of my basket, but I was too quick for them. I let out a sigh of relief as I squirmed through the hole I'd made earlier.

The noise reached EE. He jumped to his feet. 'What's going on?'

'There's a rabbit on the loose!' panted the inspector as he hurried past. 'It hasn't got a ticket!'

EE went pale. His eyes slid towards his feet. 'Really?'

Susie leaned forwards and peered under the seat. 'It's not Harriet, Dad. She's right here.'

EE watched the furious ticket inspector searching under the seats and barking questions at the other passengers. Then he looked down at me suspiciously. I did my best to look innocent, but EE didn't seem convinced.

The train began to slow down as it pulled into a station. 'Gosh, are we here already?' he said, dropping his coat over my basket to hide me. 'Come on, Susie, time to get off.'

'But this isn't our stop!' Susie said, a confused look on her face.

Gritting his teeth, EE folded up his newspaper. 'It is now.'

We had to wait an hour for another train and EE didn't stop moaning the whole time. 'I'm going to need a holiday when all this is over,' he said, staring at me over the top of his paper. 'And Harriet is paying for it.'

He had a blooming cheek – if anyone deserved a break it was me. Who was doing all the hard work around here, anyway?

CHAPTER EIGHT

Lights, Camera, Action!

By the time we got to the *Superpets* studio, EE was red-faced and puffing. And when Gloria Goodwood appeared, he got even redder.

'All the other pets are already here,' Gloria said, peering into my basket. 'We were beginning to think you'd got lost.'

68

'Bit of bother with Harriet on the train,' EE panted.

Gloria frowned. 'I hope she's OK. She's got a busy afternoon ahead of her.'

'Harriet's fine,' EE said, throwing me a grim look. I stared calmly back and washed the last of the train dust from my whiskers.

'Good.' Gloria smiled. 'Let's get her into make-up, then.'

✿ ✿ ✿

I don't mind telling you I was nervous once it was my turn to hop in front of the judges. We'd seen all kinds of amazing animals, including a counting kitten and a lizard who laughed at his owner's jokes. Then, suddenly, the cameras turned on me and the audience went quiet, waiting and watching. It was the biggest moment of my life and I didn't want to mess it up. What if I did a perfect flip, but fluffed the landing? What if – horror of horrors – I couldn't backflip at all? With my heart beating

loud in my ears, I launched myself into the air.

I needn't have worried. The *ooohs* and *aaahs* of the crowd as I landed told me I'd pulled off a fantastic flip. The judges loved it too and voted me into the next round, the quarter-finals, along with Cherry the counting kitten. She was

nice in a weird way but, boy, did she like numbers. If it moved, she counted it. Actually, even if it didn't move, she counted it. Like I said, nice but weird.

Susie was even more excited than I was that I'd made it into the quarter-finals. 'Isn't it great, Dad? Harriet's going to be a star!'

'Maybe,' EE said in his grumpiest voice. 'One thing's for certain, though. I'm never getting on another train with that rabbit. Next time, we're definitely taking the car!'

So, the next week, we drove to the studio and spent an hour trying to find a parking space. Once again, we arrived with EE looking like he'd just run a marathon.

'Deary me,' trilled Gloria, when EE gasped out the story. 'Why on earth didn't you park in the studio car park? It's right next door.'

This time I was up against a dancing

donkey and a hula-hooping chimpanzee, but they didn't stand a chance against my gymnastics. Cherry was there too, still counting. This time the people watching at home were voting for their favourite pet and after the telephone

votes had been added up, Gloria turned to the camera.

'It's been close, but only two pets can go through to the *Superpets* semi-final.'

Susie stroked my cheek. 'Paws crossed, Harriet!'

Gloria turned towards us. 'Those two pets are . . . Lulu the Chimp and Harriet Houdini!'

Susie jumped up and down with happiness beside me. I sat back, pleased I'd made it through and dreaming of the juicy carrot I was going to celebrate with. Next stop, the semi-finals!

CHAPTER NINE

Dirty Tricks

From the moment we arrived at the studio (on time!) for the semi-final, things felt different. There were a lot of new pets and their owners didn't smile at each other. Some of the animals were OK, but there was one who made it clear she didn't like me – Doodle the opera-singing Poodle. I recognised her straight away from the shows I'd watched at home. As we waited for the cameras to start rolling, I hopped up to her to say hello. She looked scornfully down at me for a minute, then pointed her long, thin nose in the air as though there was a bad smell under it.

'Get away from my Doodle, you dirty little bunny!' cried her owner, Miranda, a look of horror on her face. 'She might catch something!'

The cheek of it! The only thing Doodle had a chance of catching from me was my fabulous sense of style. But, from that moment on, it was war.

And when the results of the semi-finals were announced, and it turned out that Doodle and I would be facing each other again in the final, Doodle and Miranda did everything they could to stop me from getting there.

'Congratulations, Susie,' Miranda said

in a sickly sweet voice. 'Now, you do know the final isn't at this studio?'

'Isn't it?' Susie said, looking confused.

'Oh, no,' Miranda said. 'It's being held on the other side of the city.'

Luckily, Gloria walked past at that exact moment.

'I'm afraid you're wrong about that,' she said, with a sunny smile. 'It's going to be right here. Imagine if you'd both ended up in the wrong place!'

Miranda and Doodle waited until she'd gone to scowl at each other.

'Time for Plan B,' Miranda snarled.

They hung around until they thought no one was looking. Then Miranda rummaged in her bag and pulled out a plastic bottle. Quick as a flash, she swapped it with my bottle of shampoo, just as EE wandered up.

'So lovely to meet you,' she gabbled, grabbing his hand and pumping it up and down. 'We'd love to stay but Doodle needs her beauty sleep.'

'I expect we'll see you at the final,' EE said.

'Not if we see you first,' Miranda said, narrowing her eyes. 'But, here's a word of advice before I go. That rabbit needs a bath before the final.'

She and Doodle flounced away. EE watched them go suspiciously and then picked up the bottle Miranda had swapped for mine.

'Hair remover? What a nasty trick! No wonder Miranda was so keen for Harriet to clean up!'

I gnashed my teeth angrily. So, Doodle and Miranda wanted to fight dirty, did they? I could play that game too!

CHAPTER TEN

A Splashing Time

You wouldn't believe how hot it was in the packed television studio at the final. There wasn't a spare seat anywhere and the lights were so strong I had to have an umbrella, like the ones at the beach on holiday. I even thought about wearing sunglasses, but decided not to. I might be about to become the nation's favourite bunny, but I didn't want to be the sort of stuck-up star that no one liked.

'I wish everyone was as well behaved as you, Harriet,' the make-up lady said as she dabbed powder on to my nose. '*Some* people think they're the bee's knees.'

I tried hard not to sneeze as the dust tickled my nostrils. I knew exactly who she meant – Doodle and Miranda. I'd heard terrible stories about them afterour last meeting. They refused to get out of their limo unless a red carpet was rolled all the way out to the door.

83

And Miranda had even demanded that
Doodle had her fur restyled so that
their hairstyles matched. By the end it
was hard to tell which one was the dog
and which was the owner.

'Just between you and me, Doodle hates
getting wet,' the make-up lady whispered.
'She kicks up a right fuss when we try
and do her fur, I don't mind telling you.'

I waggled my ears thoughtfully. So, the silly poodle was scared of water, was she? I'd been looking for a way to get my own back on Doodle and her nasty owner and the make-up lady had given me an idea. All I needed was the right moment to carry it out.

It came just after the last pet had performed. Gloria was talking to Trevor and his terrific, tumbling terrapins, who weren't a patch on my crowd-pleasing triple backflip. True, the terrapins were great at tumbling, but had they spun high in the air and rung a bell above their head like I had? No, they had not.

'Phone lines will be opening in a moment.' Gloria said, turning from Trevor and beaming into the camera. 'If you'd like to see Trevor's pets every week on *Superpets,* vote terrapins.'

Next to my velvet-covered table, Doodle was sitting on her pink, satin chair beside the terrapin pool. As the cameraman zoomed in on Trevor lifting his pets out of the water, Doodle leaned towards me and bared her teeth in an unfriendly growl. As she opened her jaws to give me a nasty nip, I saw my chance. Leaping high into the air, I flipped gracefully over and pushed out with my back legs. They thumped against the legs of Doodle's chair. The chair wibbled and wobbled, sending Doodle toppling sideways. The audience gasped as she splashed into the pond with a loud yelp.

The roar of laughter from the crowd was deafening. Water flew in every direction as Doodle splashed about. Eventually she got all four paws on the bottom of the pond and stood panting, with stringy weeds dangling from her nose and her normally curly fur lying flat over her eyes.

Miranda rushed forwards, curly hair quivering. 'She tried to kill Doodle!' she screeched, pointing a shaking finger at me.

Smiling at the cheering audience, Gloria shook her head. 'I'm sure it was an accident. Harriet has obviously learned a new trick.'

Miranda's eyes narrowed. 'I demand that Harriet is disqualified!'

'I think that's up to the viewers,' Gloria said firmly. She held a hand up to her ear. 'I'm being told that the phone lines have opened. Vote now for your favourite pet!'

✿ ✿ ✿

It wasn't long before the votes were in and Gloria had lined us and our owners up on the stage once more. Miranda had tried to brush Doodle's fur, but I could still see green bits amongst her soggy curls.

'And the winner of the *Superpets Search for a Superstar* is . . .' Gloria waited for the drum roll to finish, 'Harriet Houdini!'

As I celebrated with an enormous leap and the Wilsons rushed towards Susie, Miranda grabbed the poodle's lead.

90

'Come on, Doodle. We're leaving.'

Gloria gave Susie a big hug. 'Congratulations, Susie! I'm looking forward to seeing a lot more of this talented rabbit, although I think she's earned a new name.' She looked down at me and winked. 'How does "Harriet Houdini – Stunt Bunny" grab you?'

Ooh, I liked the sound of that. I really did.

CHAPTER ELEVEN
The Great Maldini Comes Calling

Now that I was on *Superpets* every week, I had hundreds of fans. With their flashing, furry bunny ears and 'We Love Stunt Bunny' T-shirts it was hard to miss them and they were soon coming to the house at all hours. EE wasn't happy, but he could hardly send them away. What can I say? It's tough being famous.

'We might as well leave the front door open,' he said, a bad-tempered look on his face, 'or start charging people to come in.'

Susie rolled her eyes. 'Harriet is a TV star, Dad. Of course people want to meet her.'

'How did they find out where we live? That's what I want to know.'

It didn't take a genius to work out that word had got round after the final. Any day now I was expecting the newspapers to start taking an interest and then things would really take off.

When the doorbell rang early one Saturday morning, I didn't pay much attention. I was used to lots of people coming and going. Besides, Susie had given me a carrot for breakfast and I was busy nibbling it into a model of EE's head. Once it was finished, I was looking forward to biting its nose off. So, I was only half listening to the

conversation floating from the front door.

'I, ze Great Maldini, need a rabbit for my magic show.' The voice didn't sound English. 'And your 'Arriet ees perfect for ze job.'

My ears stood on end at the mention of my name. Another job? Surely one was enough?

'Don't I know you from somewhere?' EE said, sounding puzzled. Then he snapped his fingers. 'I've got it! You were at the church fair a few months ago.'

'No one forgets ze Great Maldini!'

EE's voice grew sharper. 'I certainly haven't forgotten how grumpy you were.'

The Great Maldini gave a nervous laugh. 'Eet was a hot day, we were all – 'ow you say – feeling cross-patches. But zat ees all in ze past. Today, I am 'ere for ze Stunt Bunny.'

EE thought it over. 'We're busy enough ferrying Harriet to and from the TV studio, Mr Maldini. I don't think we can take on any more work.'

'You don't understand, Signor Wilson. I want to buy your bunny. Name your price!'

I shuffled uneasily, waiting to hear EE's reply. I didn't want a new owner. Susie would be sad. I'd miss her terribly too, along with Mrs Wilson, Lily and Smudge. I'd even miss EE the *tiniest* bit. Would he see that, though?

'I'm afraid she's not for sale,' he said firmly. 'As much as I wish she was.'

'Signor Wilson, everything ees for sale. 'Ow about five thousand pounds?'

There was a long silence. My heart pounded uncomfortably.

'That's a lot of money. It would pay

for our holiday to Spain next month.' I could almost hear EE's brain whirring. 'But the answer is still no.'

'Ten thousand!' the Great Maldini cried. 'Twenty thousand! I must 'ave zat rabbit!'

This time, EE's voice had an edge of annoyance to it. 'I'm sorry, Mr Maldini, you cannot buy Harriet.'

'Zis ees not over,' the Great Maldini said, sounding angry, 'you 'ave not heard ze last of ze Great Maldini!'

There was a loud bang as the front door slammed shut. I went back to munching my carrot and decided to leave EE's nose on his face for the time being.

'Who was that?' Susie's mum asked as she came into the kitchen with a pile of freshly washed clothes and Lily trailing behind her.

'A famous magician, so he said,' EE sniffed. 'He wanted to buy Harriet to use in his show.'

Lily's eyes went wide. 'Bad man!'

Mrs Wilson patted her hand. 'Don't worry, Lily, I'm sure Daddy said no. Harriet is part of the family now.'

'Of course I did. It was tempting, though.' I heard EE sigh. 'This place gets more like a circus every day. We really should think about charging admission.'

CHAPTER TWELVE
Sitting Pretty

I was looking forward to the family summer holiday. *Superpets* had finished filming for the summer break and a week in sunny Spain sounded like the perfect way to relax. I could picture myself on a beach, sunglasses on my nose and a cool drink in my paw.

So, imagine my disgust when I found out that I was being left behind to be bunny-sat by the Greens from next door. Don't get me wrong, Mrs Green and George are very nice, but it hardly seemed fair that the rest of my family were off sunbathing while I was stuck in rainy old Britain. How would they like it if I did the same to them? Smudge was at home too, of course, but he didn't really count. I mean it's not like he needs a holiday from all his whisker-washing and cat-naps! Not like me and my busy schedule.

On the plus side, George wasn't as clued up as Susie about leaving the hutch door open. He was used to dealing with his goldfish, who was hardly likely to escape. I couldn't believe my luck when George went into the kitchen to fill up my water bottle and left me with a clear path down to the flowerbeds and EE's yummy new rosebushes. Things got even better when he tried to catch me. We had a lovely game of hide-and-seek as I scampered between the roses and the shed. After he disturbed Smudge's

sunbathing for the third time, he finally gave up and called for his mum over the garden fence.

'*Please* come out now, Harriet,' Mrs Green said, once she'd abandoned her washing up to come and help. They both peered into the shed. 'Be a good bunny,' she begged.

I ignored her. There was an interesting pile of rubber coils to keep me busy, just right for nibbling on. After an hour

or so I started to feel bad. Mrs Green and George were sitting on the steps to the house, looking very sorry for themselves. I hopped up and nudged Mrs Green's hand, before jumping back into the hutch with a *swish* of my cotton-wool tail.

'Got you!' she exclaimed, slamming the door shut behind me.

They looked so proud that I let them believe that they'd cleverly trapped me. After all, I wanted to make sure they came back to feed me the next day, didn't I? And someone had to read me my fan mail.

I suppose you think I played Mrs Green and George up every day? Well, I didn't. The rest of the week I was very well behaved, except when I *accidentally* chewed the hem of Mrs Green's skirt. It had flowers all over it, for heaven's sake. What did she expect me to think?

Even so, I think they were both looking forward to handing the front-door key back to Susie's mum and retiring from the bunny-minding business. Mrs Green certainly wasn't ready for a case of rabbit-napping.

It was the day Susie and the rest of the family were due home. Mrs Green was giving my hutch a clean before they arrived. I was safely locked away in the old cat basket, which had shiny, new plastic straps on it and a patch on the back from my great train escape. So far, I wasn't having much luck chewing my way out, but I was doing my best.

Brrrring! The sound of the doorbell made me prick up my ears. Mrs Green went to answer it.

A minute later, she was leading a tall, thin man through to the garden, a puzzled frown on her face.

'I'm sure Mr and Mrs Wilson didn't mention you'd be coming,' she said. 'Are you sure Harriet needs her claws clipped?'

107

The man smiled. 'Zey probably forgot. Ze excitement of going on holiday, no?'

I twitched my nose, thinking hard. That voice was familiar, but where had I heard it before? And what was that rubbish about my claws being clipped? The vet had only just done them. Something fishy was going on.

Smudge wandered in from the garden. He didn't trust the stranger anymore than I did because his ears flattened against his head and he let out a loud hiss.

'Well, I suppose you wouldn't be here otherwise.' Mrs Green lifted up my basket and passed it to the man. 'Do

you need to take Smudge as well?'

The man glanced down at the spitting
Smudge and shuddered.

'No, just ze rabbit.' He peered into
through the bars, dark eyes glittering.
'Come along, 'Arriet. Time to work my
magic on you!'

My eyes went wide. I'd know that curly,

black moustache anywhere. He was no claw-clipper. He was the Great Maldini and he had come to steal me away! Somehow, I had to warn Mrs Green. But how?

CHAPTER THIRTEEN
Trusty Teeth to the Rescue

I was in deep droppings. The Great Maldini
was carrying me down the garden path
and Mrs Green hadn't noticed my laid-
back ears and frantic squeaking.
And even though Smudge was doing
his best to stop the magician from
leaving, there was only so much hissing

and winding between legs that he could do. As Maldini strode towards a shiny, red car, Mrs Green waved him off and it seemed she was going to be no help at all. I was on my own.

With new determination, I started chomping on the straps holding the basket door shut. I'd chewed through them once before, I could do it again. But the new straps were strong and hurt my teeth. Seconds ticked by. The Great Maldini reached into his pocket and pulled out his car keys.

Then I heard a familiar voice. 'Harriet!'

It was Susie. I looked up to see her running along the pavement towards me, her face twisted in horror. The Great Maldini saw her too. In a flash, he'd pushed the cat basket through the open window and on to the front seat of the car. He dashed around to the driver's side. Time was running out. I chewed as though my life depended on it. Which it did, sort of.

Gnash, gnash! With a final bite of my trusty teeth, the plastic strap gave way. I pushed my nose against the basket door and wriggled through the gap.

Not a moment too soon! The Great Maldini had started the engine.

It *vroomed* into life with a great roar and the car started to roll along the road. I scrambled on top of the basket and stared at Susie's tearful face through the open window.

'Harriet, come back!' she cried.

The Great Maldini glanced over at me, grinning in triumph. 'Eet ees too late, little rabbit. Even ze Stunt Bunny cannot escape zis time!'

The car picked up speed. I looked at the grass *whizzing* by and gulped. It was now or never. I was about to perform the biggest stunt of my life.

Closing my eyes, I leaped through the open window and cartwheeled through the air. One spin, two spins, three spins . . . for one heart-stopping moment I thought I'd got it wrong.

Then I landed with a *thud* in Susie's arms.

She hugged me tightly. 'Oh, Harriet! I thought I'd lost you.'

EE arrived behind her and shook his fist at the vanishing car of the Great Maldini.

'I'm calling the police, you madman!'

I didn't think I'd ever be glad to see EE, but I was so relieved to be safe with Susie and my family that even seeing his face was wonderful! My heart slowed down as Susie carried me back into the house. I nuzzled my velvet nose against her neck, for once happy to be going back to my hutch. It had been close but, in the end, Susie had timed her return from holiday just right. And it seemed that my stunt-bunny training had saved me too!

CHAPTER FOURTEEN

The Final Bite

I have to hand it to the police. They took the attempted bunny-napping very seriously and caught the Great Maldini red-handed trying to hide our cat basket in his own shed. I don't know why he thought he'd get away with stealing the most famous rabbit in the country, but he actually did me a favour. EE bought me a swish new basket that was just the thing for a rising celebrity. Smudge tried to pretend he wasn't bothered, but I could tell by the flick of his tail that he was green with envy.

The number of people visiting the house doubled when news of my dramatic car jump reached my fans. Susie's mum began to nag EE about the state of the house and he found himself up to his grumpy eyeballs in DIY.

'We really should paint the front door,' she said, tapping her face thoughtfully. 'And the grass is far too long.'

'But the football is on,' EE grumbled. 'Can't the front door wait?'

Mrs Wilson got that look she gets when she wants her own way. 'No, it can't.'

Muttering darkly, he tramped down to the shed. Sounds of banging and clattering floated up the garden. Minutes later, he came out, trying to look disappointed.

'Oh, dear. It seems someone has nibbled through the lawnmower cable,' he sighed, gazing down at the black tube in his hands. 'And I was so looking forward to cutting the grass.'

I put on my most innocent expression.

I remembered chewing on *something* down in the shed. It didn't mean it was my fault the lawnmower didn't work. Anyone could have done it, right? Come to think of it, hadn't I seen Smudge creeping out of there yesterday, with a very guilty look on his face?

Susie's mum frowned. 'You can start

Look
out

painting the front door, then.'

EE sighed again, even louder. 'That's
the other thing. All the paintbrushes

have been eaten too. So, it looks like I can't do that job, either.'

Well, how was I meant to know they were for painting? They were just the thing for getting bits of food out of my teeth. I hopped to the back of my hutch, trying to make myself very small. EE was sure to be in a bad mood with me when he walked past.

Imagine my surprise when a crunchy, fresh carrot appeared in my cage minutes later. EE bent down and grinned through the bars at me. 'Nice one, Harriet. Now I can watch the football in peace.'

He walked into the house, whistling

a cheerful tune. I settled down to chomp on my carrot. It was tough being 'Harriet Houdini – Stunt Bunny', but someone had to do it!

Acknowledgements

Massive thanks to my husband, Lee, and my daughter, Tania, for indulging my addiction to furry friends, to Very Special Agent Jo Williamson for finding Harriet the perfect home and to Pat Posner for being the loveliest early reader ever. Lastly, thanks to Venetia, Jane and the amazing team at Simon and Schuster, who made Stunt Bunny what she is today; you guys rock!